I0649689

Fish Bone

Coldest winter

Introduction

Last summer I went
to the beach, me and
a couple of
neighborhood kids, I
guess you could say
we were like a crew,

we all lived in Rock Ridge housing projects in Gridlock City, last summer was amazing, despite the hell we lived through in our personal lives on a daily basis, when we went to the beach it was like that all faded away and we were just kids. It's amazing how one day could have such an impact in a persons life, but that was summer, and now, it's winter. My name is Kevin Brand, but everybody calls me Kave, the nickname was given to me by my sister Marissa, she's autistic and has trouble pronouncing my name, it never crossed my mind to correct her because I kinda liked it, for some reason it just fit. Even though we aren't related by blood I was raised with her and to me she was my sister, her mom was a junky who was friends with my mom, when she died of an overdose my mom took her daughter in, the irony that my mom was given custody of a junkies kid and she's a drug addict herself, but hey this is Gridlock City where even the slums have slums. Life always sucked, but it wasn't until this fall my mom found out she was dying of cancer. Sometimes I wish I could go back to that summer, when I was a kid, even if my life wasn't perfect, even if I hated every second of everyday, I never hated myself, not back then, back before she looked at me like a monster.

Episode 1
Runaway

It was late that night, the night she decided to walk back into my life. Stephanie Chapel, but everyone called her Church Girl because of her last name, I always had a crush on her but she was so shy and innocent, sometimes I would watch her and think she was the only pure and good thing in this city besides my sister, so I never told her how I felt, apart of me wanted her to stay pure, even if that meant she needed to stay away from me. She knocked on my door, well not my door, at the time I was at my bosses apartment, Stone Face Chris, he ran a gang called the Easter Island Boyz and my housing projects were their headquarters, I had just started working for him a few weeks earlier and quickly went from look out, to corner boy, and now I was getting my own pack and block to hustle on. Chris told me he never seen someone with as much ambition as I had, no one other than him that is. When I opened the door Stephanie was the last person I ever expected to see, how did she even know I was here? And more importantly, why was she even here? Last summer she drops a bomb on me at the beach, telling me she liked me, I was so caught off guard I froze, and she kissed me, that was the last day of summer, and the last day I saw her until that night. I looked for her at school, tried calling her and texting, I even reached out to her on social media, and nothing, no response, she ghosted me, we were friends for years and she vanished without a trace or a word, yet out of the blue she decides to track me down at a trap house.

Kave; "What are you doing here?"

Church Girl; "I ran away from home"

Kave; "Good for you, but why are you here?"

Church Girl; "I tried looking for you at your place but you weren't there, so I asked your mom and she said you were probably here"

Kave; "Is that what she said?"

Church Girl; "Well, she said you've been trying to sneak around and sell drugs, and since this is Chris's turf you would have to be with him, she wrote down the apartment number for me"

Kave; "Junkies, I should have known I couldn't hide shit from her for long"

Church Girl; "So it's true? Your a drug dealer?"

Kave; "I'm a survivor, I don't see anyone else trying to feed my sister or pay the bills so she can have a roof over her head"

Church Girl; "I know that, it's just"

Kave; "Just what? You breeze out of my life unexpected, then just think you can breeze back in and judge me? Fuck you, now why don't you get back to running away from home"

I shut the door in her face, I don't know why I was so angry, was it because she left? Or because she was staring at me with those judgmental eyes? Those eyes that said, your to good for this Kave, you shouldn't be doing this, like I don't fucking know that, like I wanted this. I needed to go after her, I wanted to apologize and tell her how I really felt, that I was upset when she just disappeared, I wanted to know what was going on with her and why she was running away from home, but I couldn't, I wasn't the same kid I was before she left, and I couldn't let her

come between me
and my
responsibilities.
Wolfgrin Rd stretched
through the center of
Old Wood Cove
which was my
neighborhood, at its
center was the
projects which was
split between the east
side of Rock Ridge
housing projects and
the west, the Easter

Island Boyz ran the east and a smaller crew known as the Dice Club ran the west, a truce was set between these two gangs which insured both would be safe in the center of Old Wood, however the borders of Wolfgrin Rd aren't that safe, on the north end we were at war with

Gridlock Mafia the largest gang in the city, and on the south we were at war with, the Heavy Traffic Crew which was the second largest gang in the city, location was everything, we were smaller than both gangs but with only one major road running through our neighborhood and all other backstreets protected, we were untouchable, don't get me wrong the weekly skirmish was expected, our enemies would hit us, and we would hit back, but a full on war with us would be suicide for our enemies. I was given Marsh Point, the south side of Wolfgrin Rd, the frontlines of the war with the Heavy Traffic Crew, apart of me was afraid, but the thought of making enough money to give my sister the life she deserved was enough for me to make up my mind to do it. Chris gave me a brick of dope, street value 25 grand, his cut 10 grand flat for the brick and 25% off what I made slinging, the deal was too good to be true, after bussin down the brick and cutting it, I could stretch it twice even three times over and still be at 45% purity, I was looking at 100 grand or more, even after giving Chris his cut I would have more money than I ever dreamed of. I put the brick in my book bag and started to head home, my building was just a few buildings away from Chris's so it wasn't far, but I was still on guard walking home with an annual salary in my book bag. When I got out to the courtyard I saw Church Girl being harassed by a junkie, at first it seemed he was just begging her for change, but when I saw him reach out and grab her arm I lost it, I reached behind my back into the waistband of my jeans and pulled out my big 40 caliber Glock I nicknamed "Act Right" cause whenever I pulled it out people tended to act right. I ran up on the junkie and pressed my gun to the back of his head, and lo and behold, he started to act right, as he begged me not to kill him, I couldn't find a reason not to, I was initially upset he grabbed Church Girls arm but that wasn't why I wanted to kill him, it was just, I felt like his life was meaningless, and that started to scare me, who had I become? Or what was I becoming that I felt I could take a human life so frivolously? Before I knew it Church Girl had her hand on my wrist and lowered my hand away from the junkies head, as he ran away

I couldn't help but realize how close I was to crossing a line that there would be no coming back from.

Church Girl; "Are
you ok?"

Kave; "I'm perfect,
what are you still
doing here?"

Church Girl; "I was
waiting for you"

Kave; "Why?"

Church Girl; "I still needed to talk to you"

Kave; "What could we possibly have to talk about?"

Church Girl; "Last summer"

Kave; "What about it?"

Church Girl; "I still feel the same way I did that summer, that's why I came back"

Kave; "A lot has changed since last

summer, I'm not the
guy I was back then"

Church Girl; "Your
eyes have changed,
this city can do that to
people, but you're still
the same guy who
used to cheat off my
test in middle school"

Kave; "Funny, but you're wrong, that guy is gone, you're better off without me"

Church Girl; "I know you're probably upset with me but my father forced me to switched schools and enrolled me in an all girls church school, he was upset I snuck out to go to the beach that summer, and he knew it was so I could be with you"

Kave; "So you didn't just ghost me?"

Church Girl; "Of course not, look you have your shit and I have mine, everyone does, nobodies life is perfect but we make the best of what we've got"

Kave; "And what do we have? In this hell hole of a city where the only way to escape is death or prison, what do we have?

Church Girl; "We have each other,

family and friends, and when we don't even have that, then.."

Kave; "Then what?"

Church girl; "Then we have hope, that this city is the problem and not the world as a whole, that way finding happiness is as simple as making it out this city, even if it isn't that simple"

Her words were childish, but we were kids, so maybe that's why I wanted to believe her, I wanted to believe that the people in my life were enough for me, and that I could be enough for them, and maybe, just maybe we could all make it out this city.

Kave; "Maybe you're right, maybe we can make it out this city, or maybe we shouldn't have to, maybe I don't wanna run"

Church Girl; "Its not running, its…"

Kave; "Its what? This is my city, I don't need to run"

Church Girl; "So this is your city now?"

Kave; "Yeah, I'm starting to think it is"

I don't know why I was saying what I was saying, all I wanted was to get out this city a few months ago, but now shit was different, I had a real shot at getting money, I couldn't run now, run and do what? Be broke living on the streets or some dumb shit, this girl was living in a fucking fantasy, all I needed was my gun and this pack, and I was about to be on.

Kave; "You should go, theres nothing here for you, but as for me, yeah, this is my fucking city"

Church Girl; "Then its my city too"

Kave; "What are you talking about?"

Church Girl; "If you wanna stay then I will to, I'm enrolled in Hejaku academy for girls, now you know"

Kave; "Hejaku academy? And here I thought your father

belonged to the
church of Sedeneve"

Church Girl;
"Thats not funny"
   Kave; "It wasn't
meant to be, that man
has been an asshole
since…"

   Church Girl; "Shut
up! My dad may be
strict but he is a great

man and a great father"

Kave; "And yet his little girl wants to run away"

Church Girl; "You don't know shit ok"

Kave; "Geez, relax, it was just a joke"

Church Girl; "I made a choice, and I

chose you, thats why I wanted to run away"

Kave; "Me? Listen…"

Church Girl; "Save it, I don't need to hear how you're not worth it, you, our friends, your sister, you all mean everything to me"

Kave; "So where are you going now?"

Church Girl; "Home I guess"

It was late so I decided to walk her home, unfortunately that meant leaving my hood, she lived deep in HTC territory, lowkey I wasn't that known yet so I figured

I should be cool. Four blocks away from her house and some lame ass HTC pussies pull up on us in some dusty ass mini van, I ain't have time for these broke mother fuckers, but shit was what it was.

Bitch driving; "Fuck you doin over here hoe ass boy, ion know you"

Kave; "Ain't no hoe in me nigga, we can rock out, fuck you tryna do?"

Shit wasn't gonna cool off, these niggas was wit it, so fuck was I supposed to do? I upped my Glock and started dumpin, after emptying the clip, I knew they were all

dead, shit was crazy,
my heart was racing,
the smell of gun
powder and blood
was intoxicating, it
was such a fucking
rush, these niggas was
talking all that hot shit
and now they swiss
cheesed in a fucking
mini van, I couldn't
help but laugh, when
I looked at church
girl, she was afraid,

the way she looked at me, like I was Sedeneve himself, I tried to speak to her but she just ran, I didn't have time to chase her, I had to get the fuck away from the crime scene, so I started to run back to my hood. Before I knew it I was at Marsh point, home sweet fucking home, I could relax a bit, so I took my time walking back to my projects, I couldn't get what happened out my head, three kills in one night, not to mention it was my first time killing anyone, I felt like I could do anything, I felt powerful. After getting back to my building I went up to my apartment, the electricity was off again, luckily there was no food in the fridge to worry about, this was my motivation, my mom dying while still getting high in a dark project apartment while my sister is in her room and more than likely went to bed hungry, but this was all gonna change, I was gonna fix everything. I must have passed out, when I woke up there was banging at my door, Chris and two of his goons decided to pay me a visit about what went down in HTC territory.

Stone face Chris;
"What the fuck Kave?
Word on the street
you killed a couple of
HTC punks out
south"

Kave; "Shit got messy, you know how it go"

Stone face Chris; "Nigga are you crazy, this shit could start a war lil nigga"

Kave; "Lil nigga? Nah homie, as of last night I ain't no lil nigga"

Shit was getting spicy, I had respect for Chris for putting me on but bro needed to watch his tone, I started feeling like shit could go left so I made my way over to my book bag where I had my gun, and thats when he said what I ain't want him to say, what I knew I would kill him for saying.

Stone face Chris; "Yeah aight lil nigga, imma need that pack back, you ah dub in these streets, no movements"

Kave; "Oh word, bet bro, its right here in my bag"

As soon as I reached into the bag I backed out my glizzo and let that shit go, well thats what was supposed to happen, but last night I never changed clips,

my shit was empty,
that moment felt like
an eternity, I stood
there glizzo upped for
no reason, watching
these niggas back out
on me, when they
started dumpin I
knew I was dead, I
could feel the shots
ripping through me,
they lit my ass up, but
fuck it, this was the
game. As I laid there

bleeding I watched them go through my bag and take my only shot at a future, my way of taking care of my sister, and that hurt worse than any bullet. I blacked out, when I came to, a week had passed and I was in the hospital, It felt like I was at the beach again, cause all my niggas was there,

Rayshaun aka Razor, bro always got a blade on him, Tayvon aka Lint, boy ain't never got no money, and Bryan aka Blue Nose, bro was like a pitbull when he fought, once he got on yo ass wasn't no getting him off, this was my crew, we grew up together, but shit changed.

Kave; "Is my mom here?"

Razor; "Nah bro, she probably home wit ya sister"

Blue Nose; "Or out getting high"

Lint; "Blue, thats his moms chill"

Blue Nose; "Chill? My nigga stretched out in the hospital and this bitch ain't here"

Kave; "Relax, Blue right, but I ain't stretched out nigga, if I was that would mean I'm dead, dumbass lil boy"

Blue Nose; "Oh you tough now, was you tough when niggas aired ya bitch ass out?"

Kave; "Nigga got all the jokes I see, ha ha ha"

Razor; "Nah nigga, the time for joking is over, what we doin?"

Kave; "Isn't it obvious? Its war"

And like that, it was what it was, and it was war.

To be continued…

www.ingramcontent.com/pod-product-compliance
Lightning Source LLC
Chambersburg PA
CBHW051527050726
47503CB00014B/2189